Ophelia's Shadow Theatre

by Michael Ende

with Illustrations by
Friedrich Hechelmann

Translated from the German
by Anthea Bell

The Overlook Press

There was once a little old lady called Ophelia who lived in a little old town.

When she was born – and that was a long time ago – her parents had said: »One of these days our daughter will be a great star actress.«
So they had given her the name of a famous character in a play.
Little Miss Ophelia had inherited her parent's love of the beautiful language of the poets, but that was all. And she couldn't be a famous actress, because her voice was too quiet. However, she wanted to devote her life to art somehow, in her own small way.

There was a pretty theatre in the little old town. On the very edge of the stage, where the people in the audience couldn't see it, stood a box. Miss Ophelia used to sit in this box every evening whispering the words of the actors' parts to them, in case they got stuck.
Of course, her quiet voice was just right for that, since the audience wasn't supposed to hear her at all.
Miss Ophelia had been doing this job all her life, and she enjoyed it. Bit by bit, she learned all the great comedies and tragedies of the world off by heart, until she didn't even need to look at the books of the plays.

But now Miss Ophelia was old, and times had changed. Fewer and fewer people came to see plays in the theatre in the little old town, for there were films and television and other amusements these days. Most of them had cars, and if they ever did want to go to the theatre they preferred to drive to the nearest big city, which was a much grander place to be seen in, and where they could watch far more famous actors.
So the theatre in the little old town was closed, the actors went away, and little old Miss Ophelia lost her job too.

When the last performance was over, and the curtain had fallen for the last time, she stayed behind in the theatre for a little while all on her own. She sat in her box and thought of her past life. Suddenly she saw a shadow flitting in and out of the wings, growing sometimes larger and sometimes smaller. But there was nobody there to cast it. »Hello!« said Miss Ophelia, in her quiet voice. »Who's there?« The shadow was obviously alarmed, and it shrank. It had no definite shape anyway. But then it pulled itself together and grew again. »Sorry!« it said. »I didn't know there was anyone still here. I didn't mean to frighten you. I only came in because I've nowhere else to go. Please don't chase me away.«
»Are you a shadow?« asked Ophelia.
The shadow nodded.

»But a shadow must belong to someone,« she went on.

»No,« said the shadow, »not all of us do. There are a few extra shadows about the place who don't belong to anyone, and nobody
wants them. I'm one of those. My name is Shady.«

»Oh,« said Miss Ophelia. »Isn't it sad for you, not having anyone of
your own?«

»Very sad,« the shadow said, sighing softly, »but what can I do about
it?«

»Would you like to come and live with me?« asked the old lady.
»I don't have anyone of my own either.«

»I'd love to,« said the shadow. »That would be wonderful. But I'd
have to be joined to you, and you already have a shadow.«

»I'm sure you'll manage to get along together,« said Miss Ophelia.
And her own shadow nodded.

From then on, Miss Ophelia had two shadows. Not many people
noticed, but those who did were surprised, and thought it rather
strange.

Miss Ophelia didn't want people talking about her, so she used to
ask one or other of the two shadows to make itself very small in the
daytime and slip into her handbag. A shadow fits in anywhere.

One day Miss Ophelia was sitting in church, talking to the Lord God
and hoping (for she wasn't quite sure) that he was listening to her,
even though her voice was so quiet, when she suddenly saw a shadow on the white wall. It seemed to be a very thin shadow, and
although it didn't look like anything in particular, it was stretching
out an imploring hand.

»Are you another shadow who doesn't belong to anyone?« she asked.

»That's right,« said the shadow, »but we've heard there's someone
who will take us in. Would that be you?«

»I have two shadows already,« said Miss Ophelia.

»Then one more won't matter, will it?« the shadow begged.

»Couldn't you take me in too? It's so sad and lonely without anyone
of my own.«

»What's your name?« asked the old lady, kindly.

»My name is Dark Dismay,« whispered the shadow.

»Well, come along, then,« said Miss Ophelia.

So now she had three shadows.

From then on, more and more shadows who didn't belong to anyone kept turning up, almost daily, for there are a great many shadows like that in the world.

The fourth was called All Alone.

The fifth was called Peak-and-Pine.

The sixth was called Nevermore.

The seventh was called Sad-and-Sorry.

And so it went on. Old Miss Ophelia was poor, but luckily none of the shadows needed anything to eat, or clothes to keep them warm. But her little room was sometimes very dark, full of all the shadows who had come to live with her because nobody else wanted them. Miss Ophelia didn't have the heart to turn them away. And still they kept on coming.

It was worst when the shadows started quarrelling. They squabbled over the best place in the room, and they fought each other and sometimes even had shadow boxing matches. On such nights as those, little old Miss Ophelia couldn't sleep. She would lie in bed with her eyes open, trying to soothe the shadows in her quiet voice, but it didn't do much good.

Miss Ophelia did not like fights, unless they were written in the beautiful language of the poets and acted on stage, which was different. And then one day she had a good idea.

»Listen,« she told the shadows, »if you want to stay with me, there's something you must learn.«

The shadows stopped quarreling and looked expectantly at her from every corner of the little room.

Then she recited the beautiful words of the poets to them, all the words she knew off by heart. She recited some bits very slowly, telling the shadows to repeat the words after her. The shadows worked hard, and they learned fast.

So gradually little old Miss Ophelia taught them all the great comedies and tragedies of the world.

And now, of course, things were very different, since a shadow can play any part it likes: it can look like a dwarf or a giant, a man or a bird, even a tree or a table.

Night after night, they would act the most wonderful plays for Miss Ophelia. And she whispered them the words of their parts, in case they got stuck.

In the daytime, however, they all lived in Miss Ophelia's handbag – except for her own shadow, of course. For shadows can make themselves incredibly small when they like.

So other people never saw all Miss Ophelia's shadows, but they realized there was something unusual going on. And people do not like anything unusual.

»That old lady is very odd,« said some, behind her back. »She ought to be put in a Home where they'd look after her.« And others said, »Perhaps she's crazy. Goodness knows what she might do one of these days!«

And they kept well out of her way.

At last the landlord of the house where Miss Ophelia had her little room came to see her and said, »I'm sorry, but from now on you must pay twice as much rent as before.«

Miss Ophelia couldn't pay twice as much rent.

»Well then,« said her landlord, »I'm very sorry, but I think you'd better move out.«

So Miss Ophelia packed everything she owned in a suitcase – there wasn't much – and went away. She bought a ticket, got into a train and went out into the world, going she herself didn't know where. When she had travelled far enough by train, she got out and went on with her journey on foot. She carried her suitcase in one hand, and her handbag of shadows in the other.

It was a long, long journey.

At last Ophelia came to the sea, and then she could go no farther. So she sat down to rest for a while, and fell asleep. All the shadows came out of the handbag and stood around her, discussing what to do next.

»It's really our fault Miss Ophelia is in trouble,« they said.

»She helped us, and now we ought to help her. We've all learned something from her, so perhaps we can use it to do her good.«

And when Miss Ophelia woke up, they told her their plan.

»Oh,« said Miss Ophelia, »how very kind of you.«

When they came to a little village, she took a white sheet out of her suitcase and hung it over a carpet-beating pole. The shadows immediately began acting the plays Miss Ophelia had taught them against the white sheet. And she herself sat behind it, whispering the beautiful words of the poets to them, in case they got stuck.

At first no one came but a few children, who watched in wonder, but towards evening a few grown-ups turned up too, and after the show they all paid a little money for the interesting performance they had seen.

So now Miss Ophelia went from village to village and town to town, and her shadows became kings and jesters, noble ladies and fiery stallions, enchanters and flowers, whatever was needed in the play. People came to watch, and found themselves laughing and crying. Soon Miss Ophelia was famous, and wherever she went she was eagerly expected, for no one had ever seen anything like her plays before. The audience clapped and clapped, and they all paid something, some of them more and others less.

After a while Miss Ophelia had saved enough money to buy herself a little old car. She had it painted by an artist in nice bright colours, and there were big letters on both sides, saying:

OPHELIA'S SHADOW THEATRE

Now she could drive all over the world in her car, and her shadows went with her.

This might be the end of the story, but it isn't.
For one day, when Miss Ophelia had driven into a snowstorm in her car and was stuck, she suddenly saw a vast shadow looming up in front of her, a shadow much darker than all the rest.
»Are you another shadow that nobody wants?« she asked.
»Yes,« said the shadow slowly, »I think you could say so.«
»Do you want to come and stay with me too?« asked Miss Ophelia.
»Would you take me in?« asked the great shadow, coming closer.
»Well, I do have more than enough shadows already,« said the little old lady, »but you must have some place to go.«
»Don't you want to know my name first?« asked the shadow.
»What is it, then?«
»They call me Death.«
Then there was silence for quite a long time.

Ophelia

Shadow Theatre

»Will you still take me in?« asked the shadow at last, gently.
»Yes,« said Miss Ophelia, »come along.«
Then the great, cold shadow wrapped itself around her, and the whole world went dark. But suddenly she felt as if she were opening a brand-new pair of eyes, eyes that were young and clear, not old and short-sighted any more. And she didn't need glasses now to see where she was.

She was standing at the gates of Heaven, and around her stood a throng of beautiful figures in bright clothes, smiling at her.
»Who are you all?« asked Miss Ophelia.
»Don't you know us?« they said. »We're all the shadows you took in. We are free now; we needn't wander any more.«
Then the gates of Heaven opened, and the bright figures went in, taking little old Miss Ophelia with them. They led her to what looked like a wonderful palace, though it was really the finest and most magnificent theatre ever seen.
Above the entrance there were big gold letters, saying:

So ever since, Miss Ophelia's shadows have been acting tales of the fortunes of mankind for the angels in the beautiful language of the poets, for the angels know that language too, and it tells them how wretched yet wonderful, how sad yet comical it is to be human and live on Earth.

Miss Ophelia whispers her actors the words of their parts, in case they get stuck. And some say that the Lord God himself sometimes comes to watch the plays. But nobody knows for sure.

Michael Ende,
born in 1929, is one of the best-known German
authors of today. In 1981 he was awarded the
Janus-Korczak-Prize for his literary œuvre and in
1982 the international »Lorenzo il
Magnifico«-Prize. Besides his most successful
books »Momo« and »The Neverending Story« he
has written, among others, several poetic picture-
book stories.

Friedrich Hechelmann,
was born in 1948. He graduated from the
»Grafische Lehr- und Versuchsanstalt«
(Educational and Research Institute for Graphic
Arts) in Vienna where he subsequently studied at
the Academy of Fine Arts. Since 1973 he has been
living near Isny in the Allgäu as a painter and
free-lance illustrator and also makes
TV-programmes for South German
Broadcasting/ARD.
Also published by Thienemann is Friedrich
Hechelmann's picture-book »Malle der
Stolperhans« (Malle the Stumblethrush), text by
Ronald Granz, and available from the EDITION
WEITBRECHT is the collection of Stories
»Hechelmanns Lesereise« (Hechelmann's Reading
Journey), illustrated by F. Hechelmann himself,
and several other books.